D0251016

This book belongs to:

_____

For Florence Emily Hackett, with love

All Ladybird books are available at most bookshops,
supermarkets and newsagents, or can be ordered direct from:
Ladybird Postal Sales
PO Box 133 Paignton TQ3 2YP England
Telephone: (+44) 01803 554761
Fax: (+44) 01803 663394

A catalogue record for this book is available
from the British Library

Published by Ladybird Books Ltd
A subsidiary of the Penguin Group
A Pearson Company

Illustrations © Klaas Verplancke MCMXCVIII
Text © Judith Nicholls MCMXCVIII

LADYBIRD and the device of a Ladybird are trademarks of
Ladybird Books Ltd Loughborough Leicestershire UK

knock! knock!

by Judith Nicholls
illustrated by Klaas Verplancke

Ladybird

"Knock, knock!" said the chick.

"Is it a rock? Is it a brick?"

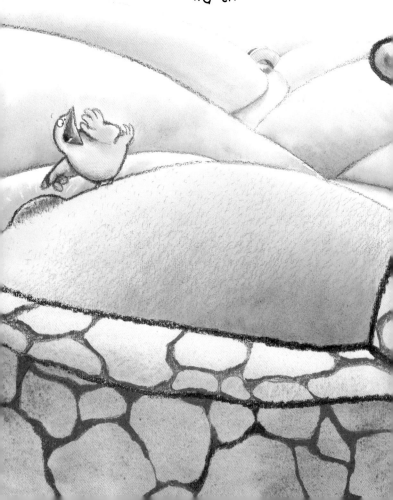

"Come here, Duck," said the chick.

"It's very still," said the chick.

"Come here, Dog!" said the duck.

"Come here, Frog!" said the chick.

"It's not *tall*," said the frog.

"It's quite small," said the frog.

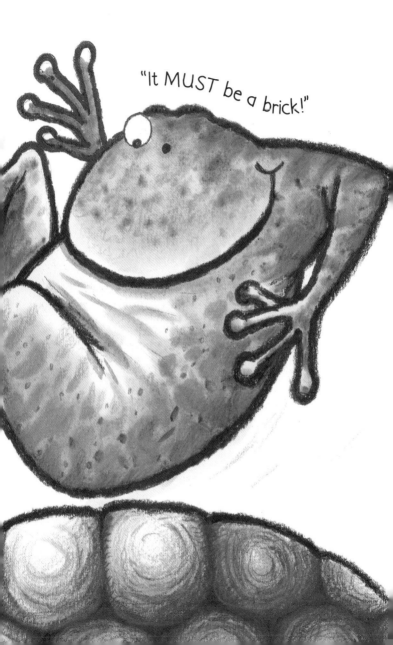

"Stand back!" said the duck.

"It's a trick!" said the chick.

"Get my stick!" said the dog.

"CHEEP, CHEEP!" said the chick.

"QUACK, QUACK!" said the duck.

"KNOCK! KNOCK!" said the dog.

"LOOK OUT!" said the frog.

tap
tap

"It IS just a brick," said the duck and the chick.

"It IS just a rock," said the dog and the frog.

But the rock said...